CHAMPAGNE Kisses

Eleanor Green

ALSO BY ELEANOR GREEN

Torn

Wait for Me (Book 1)

Stay with Me (Book 2)

Crowded

Eleanor Green

Happy New Year to you!
May every great new day
Bring you sweet surprises—a happiness buffet.
Happy New Year to you,
And when the new year's done,
May the next year be even better,
Full of pleasure, joy, and fun.

– Anonymous

CHAPTER *one*

Briley

I have just realized dorm life isn't for me. When two girls
from Alpha Chi Omega come around and pull my roommate,
Ava, from her twin bed, dragging her out of our dorm in
nothing but her minion boxers and matching tank, I also
realize I'm not sorority material. It's like being trapped in a
nightmare of monogrammed bows and ridiculous matching
sweatshirts that make no sense in the Florida heat. Maybe it's
part of initiation, seeing who can go the longest without
passing out while still looking cute.

As two more girls stalk toward my bed with their
Cheshire cat grins, I start to panic.

Raising my hands in the air, I declare, "You're too late.
Zetas already got me." It's a bold faced lie, and I hope they
don't have a way of checking. My bras will probably be
strung up the flag pole in the morning, but what choice do I
have? It was the quickest thing I could come up with at
midnight.

Two things tend to happen when I panic: I lie and I hide.

As soon as the girls' giggles have dissipated and I feel the coast is clear, I pack a few things in a duffel, sneak down the concrete hallway, into the stairwell, and toward my champagne Volkswagen Jetta.

Cooper's apartment is still lit on the inside, and it sounds like he has a few people over, so I don't hesitate to impose. I never know what I'm getting myself into when I come to his place. It's close to campus, and between him and his roommate, Colin, there's no telling what kind of crowd will be inside. I have my own key, but decide not to use it. I don't want to be *that girl,* the one that slips in whenever she pleases. Before knocking, I rest my ear against the grey metal door and hear at least two male voices. I feel sure I'm not going to break up anything romantic.

Romantic. A silent chuckle shakes my shoulders at the thought of Cooper being romantic. He's a player for sure, but never romantic. He's living it up in college. And he should, as long as he's careful.

A few taps on the door and I'm still standing there, ignored. Finally I put some power behind my fist and bang harder. Colin swings the door open, looking disappointed when he sees me.

I've only known this dude for a few months, but I feel comfortable enough to give him the eat-shit look he deserves. "Expecting strippers?"

"No," he chuckles. "Pizza."

Just when I'm about to roll my eyes at his lack of truth telling skills, the pizza guy pulls up and saves us both from an awkward moment. Maybe I've gotten the wrong impression of Colin.

I step through the door while he pays the pizza guy and see the scene before me. Cooper and two other guys I've seen before but don't remember specifically are sitting around the living room. One of them is on the arm of the couch, holding an acoustic guitar, his wavy blond hair hitting the top of his shoulders. Another is lounging on the floor with a pen and pad of paper. He has dark hair and skin and, if I recall, eyes just as dark. Coop is in his chair—a tattered blue recliner that no longer reclines—with his acoustic. He's the one that brings light to the room. Everything about him is perfect and flawless and contradictory.

My best friend is gorgeous and he knows it, but he never tries to be. He's comfortable in his skin—or the white T-shirt that clings to his muscled chest and a pair of basketball shorts—which I envy. His light brown hair always looks freshly washed and left to dry however the towel scrubbing decides.

My insides instantly warm when I see him, but not in a sexual way. He's my comfort, my home, my constant.

"Hey, B." Cooper grins and pats the arm of his broken recliner for me to take a seat. "Hungry?"

He doesn't ask me if I'm okay, or why I've come over at this late hour, because this is normal for us. I never have to ask to come crash on the couch if I need to get away from dorm life or have a quiet place to study when the guys are out. Colin hasn't complained yet, or at least I'm not aware of it if he has. Cooper has either threatened to kick his ass, or he doesn't mind because I always clean the place before I leave. These dudes are nasty, leaving their dishes un-rinsed in the sink for days, so they're getting the better end of the deal for sure.

"Nah. Just tired," I tell him, a yawn taking over my lungs and limbs."Can I crash here tonight?"

"Sure. What's up?" Coop stands, pulls a slice of pizza from the box, and stalks toward me.

"Pledge week." My upper lip pulls upward in a snarl. "The bows are out kidnapping people in their sleep tonight."

Coop shoves half the slice in his mouth, wipes the pepperoni grease from his chin with the back of his hand, talking while he chews. "I thought you were gonna give it a try?"

My head shakes as I answer, a confirmation that I'm standing firm on my decision, and my nose wrinkles up. "I don't think it's for me. I just can't wrap my head around the idea. Can you imagine me in ruffled shorts and a bow bigger than my head?" My pulse kicks up just thinking about all the things they're making those poor conformists do. "And the first time someone tells me to do something 'or else' . . ." My shoulders suddenly tense at the thought, and I have to roll my neck to relieve the stress building there. "Can you even, Coop? Wear this, do this, match us, be like us—"

"Whoa!" Cooper grips my shoulders and gives them a squeeze. His clear green eyes stare down at me, unblinking like I've just said something outrageous. "You're going to shoot right through the ceiling. Where do you get these crazy ideas?"

I feel like an idiot when I say it aloud. "*Legally Blonde?*" I present my answer in question form, dragging the title out in shame.

When Cooper snorts, I don't feel any better. I slap my hand on the light switch in his bedroom a little harder than necessary. "I know, I know," I confess, dropping my bag on the floor. "I panicked and it gets worse."

"How?" He's still laughing while he chews the last bite of pizza.

Before I answer, I tie my dark brown hair into a messy bun and secure it with two pony tail holders. It's almost to my waist, but too hot to wear it down most days. "They were about to take me . . ." My face muscles twitch, knowing I'm going to get the best-friend-that-acts-like-a-big-brother lecture. "So I told them I was already spoken for . . . by Delta Zeta." I narrow one eye as I remember. "Actually, I couldn't remember the Delta part, so I just said Zeta. Think they'll check?" I tug anxiously on the tattered Foo Fighters T-shirt I slipped on before I ran out the door.

Cooper huffs out a long breath and shakes his head. He's smirking but I can't tell if he thinks I'm ridiculous for coming up with such a lame lie or if he believes it was really great and thinks I'm super cute. I go with the latter and bite my bottom lip to play the part.

"There's only one Zeta, B, whether you say the Delta or not." The right side of his mouth pulls up, deepening that damn smirk on his face. "Pretty sure if they wanna know, they will." He cocks his head to the side, driving the point home. *You're an airhead.*

"Shit, shit, shit." My thumbnail is already chewed off, but I attempt to bite anyway.

"They could give a shit, B. Nothing to worry about." He gives me a light shove to the arm, but it's enough to knock me off balance and make me stumble. "That's why you're hiding out here?" The way he's laughing, nearly doubled over and shoulders shaking, has me on the edge of wanting to join him and wanting to bull right into him. I settle for a gut punch that doesn't faze him.

"We're going to be up late, practicing." Cooper takes a pillow off the bed. "I'll take the couch so I don't wake you." There's a weird look on his face that I can't unveil. He hesitates at the door, a pensive expression as he rubs the back of his neck. We've slept in the same bed a gazillion times, why is tonight different? I wonder if he planned to have a girl over later and I'm wrecking his plan.

I just shake my head, too tired to discuss it. While I'm digging in my bag for my toothbrush, I end with, "Whatever works. You won't wake me. I'm coma-tired."

***

The week takes it sweet time passing and thankfully there's no drama over my sorority tale. My roommate, Ava, is officially an Alpha Chi Omega, and although she's super bummed I didn't join her, she's quickly making new friends and loving that scene. I'm constantly trying to bite my tongue and hold my opinion of that world, but when she stands in front of our full length mirror taking selfies while sporting her AXΩ sweatshirt, I lose it.

"It's freaking ninety-seven degrees outside!"

She grins at me through the reflection of the mirror, her lips smacking while she chews a piece of gum. "It's December, Briley. It's like seventy-four."

Seventy-four is not cold and she knows it. "How can you stand it?" I ask, my tone harsher than I planned. "I don't mean any disrespect, truly, but do they *make* you all wear the matching stuff, or do you really like it?"

"Both." Her blasé attitude lets me off the hook for being too harsh, so I shove my ear buds in and get lost in the haunting tunes of Massive Attack.

***

As soon as you relax, that's when the bitch slap comes. At least that's what I learn on Thursday.

It's an average day, mild weather and a cloudless sky. My first stop is The Frothy Monkey for my tropical protein smoothie. I leave enough time to walk to my nine-thirty Literature class while sipping my breakfast and enjoying the feel of the sun warming my bare shoulders. I can't imagine a sweatshirt, even in this cooler season.

The University is large, but I always tend to see the same people on the way to class. As I pass Caroline Wells, she gives me a strange look, and then Nikki Tapp does the same. *Ookay.* No big deal, I guess. But by the time I sit down in Lit class and notice Bethany Lemmon raising an eyebrow in my direction, I pick up my things and move to sit next to her to get the scoop.

"It's none of my business who you date, Briley, but how drunk were you?" Bethany then proceeds to tell me everything I apparently did, with a guy I barely know, in the most ridiculous place.

Say what now?

"Roxanna told you this?" I ask, stunned and slightly horrified. Bethany nods, sucking in her lower lip. "And you believed her?" I don't wait for her response before picking up my things and leaving. The professor gives me a disapproving glance, and I'm sure the entire class is staring, but I have to get out of there.

Roxanna Talbot is a bitch. A filthy, lying bitch.

I make it back to my dorm in record time, not caring that I'm missing the review that'll give us most of the answers for Friday's test. I have to get away from everyone, think about something more than the one word on repeat in my head: *bitch, bitch, bitch!*

Tossing my backpack on the floor next to the desk, I fall back onto my bed, the crappy mattress too old and stubborn to give and accept my body. Everything around me here suddenly reminds me of home—framed pictures of family, my Hello Kitty doll, a tattered copy of Wuthering Heights— and I desperately want to run into the arms of my mother. She would hold me until I cry it out, then make me a cup of tea and put on a Vince Vaughn movie. He always makes me laugh.

But I can't run home. The semester is almost over, and I have finals. Plus, I refuse to bury my head into my silver and black striped pillowcase because I know what's beneath the fabric—the down feathers of my childhood, the same ones that have captured most of my tears—and it's right here, willing to take more, eager to comfort me. *Not yet.* I want to stay in this pissed off zone a little longer, letting the rage consume me so I don't break down.

Not yet.

Instead I call Cooper. He needs to know the truth before he goes off the deep end. But most importantly, he's my personal pocket comedian and I know he'll make it all better. He tells the dumbest jokes, but that's what makes them so funny. *"Know the difference between a women's cross country team and African pygmies? African pygmies are cunning runts."* Gets me every single time. Full on belly laugh even after the one hundred and seventeenth time hearing it.

I think I understand why Roxanna Talbot spread the rumor about me. Because I lied about the sorority and didn't let her little clan pull me into their ring. She's a bitch, that's how she rolls. Whatever. But why she connected me with Kyle Greer is beyond me. I didn't think anyone could possibly believe it. But she sure-as-shit did it, and apparently, they all sure-as-shit believe it. If anyone on this godforsaken campus would just use the brains that got them here, they'd see how foolish the rumor is. First of all, Kyle Greer is a pothead asshole. Okay, I'm *assuming* he smokes pot by the way he dresses, but he's for sure an asshole and disrespects every girl in his path. Totally not my type. Second, and most important, is the *way* I apparently got with this loser. On the front lawn. Of the Kappa Alpha house. Seriously? That's how it went down? I can barely play it out in my head.

Am I so desperate to get it on with this dude whom I've never talked to outside of Music Appreciation class that I would fling my clothes into the bushes, drop down on the itchy grass—after kicking the empty beer cans out of the way—and beg him to take me? Gah! I'm so pissed off, I don't know whether to kick Roxanna's ass or Kyle's for making this imaginary night of sex so cheap and itchy.

My trashcan sails through the air after I give it a kick, wadded tissue and a few Tootsie Pop wrappers scattering across the room before it hits and settles in front of the dorm door.

Ava comes in and nearly trips over the can. Her blond hair is pulled up high on her head in a tight ponytail. I wonder if I've missed the memo that Madonna's iconic hairstyle is back in.

"Whoa, what happened?" She braces herself with one hand against the door frame and steps over the trash pile.

My eyes roll so hard, I think I've seen what my ass looks like in these shorts. Suddenly her face changes from unknowing to realization. "I heard." Her nose crinkles and shoulders slump for an instant before she sits on the edge of her bed, facing me. "I don't see what the big deal is. My first time was in the back of my boyfriend's car. Actually, it was his dad's car. What could be worse than that?"

"Seriously?" My head does a shiver-shake like I've got a twitch from an old stroke. "It didn't happen. At all. Not on the front lawn, not anywhere." I know my expression is ridiculous, I can feel every muscle contract and distort to convey my shock and disappointment. "One, what makes you think I'm a virgin?" No way in hell she knows. "And two, Kyle Greer?" I drag out his last name. "Seriously?"

"He's not *that* terrible, Briley." She flops back onto her bed, pulling her arms behind her head for support. "Eccentric, maybe. He'll probably be one of those billionaires that we'll see on TV and you'll wish you *had* given it to him."

It takes me a minute to realize we're not talking about the same Kyle. With a shrug of the shoulder, I huff out a humorless laugh. "No, not Kyle from the fourth floor. Kyle Greer, the douche that tries to dry hump anything with legs."

She shoots up into sitting position and covers her mouth with her hand. Her eyes are wide like she's about to call out

BINGO for the prize. *Yup, that Kyle. Now you get why I'm freaked.* "Oh God, seriously?"

I nod, thankful she's caught on. "You're missing the real problem, here, though," I sigh, the worry furrowing my brows.

"What's that?"

"Cooper," I practically moan. "I haven't been able to reach him." My mind races as I pace the room. I hope he's at the dentist or somewhere that would warrant his cell phone going straight to voicemail. He always answers my calls immediately, no matter where he is. I recall the last time he answered my call and *should* have let it go to voicemail. *"Can I call you back, I'm in the bathroom."* Such a dude.

"So what?" She makes a face. "He's not your brother or your keeper." Suddenly, her brows stand at attention. "You like him, don't you? I mean, like-like him." She bobs her head from side to side.

I frown. Liking Cooper? How ridiculous. "No. I don't like-like him." I can't help mocking her head bob. "We've been friends forever. Since we were in diapers. But he's super overprotective. Like, Liam Neeson in *Taken* protective. I have to get to him before he gets to Kyle or he may never hold a joint again." It was too easy for me to picture Kyle's broken body on the front lawn of the frat house, Cooper standing over him shaking off his sore fist. Kyle has no idea why Coop just beat the shit out of him.

I've formed a rhythm for the past twenty minutes, tapping my phone's recent call list, clicking Cooper's name, and repeating that process as soon as I hear the beginning of his *"If you want me, tell me"* message. My finger is hovering over the end button when a fist slams into our thin door three times. Ava and I both jump up and stare at the door instead of answering it.

"B, it's me. Open up," Cooper's voice booms through the wood, clipped and rushed, making him sound like an insane boyfriend. Which he's not.

For an instant, I'm scared. He's never yelled at me like that, and I wonder if he's pissed at me. I swing open the door, half hurt that he could believe I would do something so cheap and stupid, and half angry that he thinks he has a say in it. Cooper's no saint. I know he's slept with at least two girls. I caught each of them sneaking out of his window one summer back home. Now that he has his own apartment, and no reason to sneak around, he's probably going through enough condoms to help pay for Trojan advertising.

I've barely gotten the door open when Cooper storms in and grips my biceps. There's desperation in his eyes, stiffness in his shoulders, and the muscles in his jaw are pulsing. "Are you okay?" He's looking me over like I've just gotten out of the hospital. I feel the tremors in his hands before I see him shaking.

"I'm fine." Pulling my arms loose, I step back and shove the door shut with my foot. "What's going on?" The way he's acting throws me off. I didn't expect him to react this way.

"I—" He shakes his head back and forth, struggling to get the words out. I want to save him, let him know the rumors aren't true, but I'm kind of curious to know what he's heard. Are the rumors getting worse? By the time they make their way around campus, I'll have had sex on the back of a horse while trotting through town.

12

"Hey," I begin, trying to calm him with my tone. "I'm fine. Sit down and tell me what you've heard." I lace my fingers through his and lead him toward my bed.

He takes one look at Ava and nods politely, huffing out a breath.

"Hi, Cooper," Ava sings as she stands and picks up her laptop. She can't take her eyes off him as she backs up toward the door. "I've got a paper to finish. Catch you guys later."

It's just the two of us after she shuts the door. "Come on, sit down." I look at his knuckles and can tell he hasn't used them on anyone. *Thank God.*

Cooper plops down next to me so hard, I sink and bang into his side. He turns to face me, his eyes wild with concern and anger. "I had to come here first to make sure you were okay. Did he hurt you? Did he force . . ." He scrubs his palms over his face. "What were you thinking going to that party, B?" He stands and turns away from me. "That son of a bitch!"

Damn it, not you too. "It's all a lie, Coop." My eyes blink closed and stay there for at least a three count as disappointment fills me.

He whirls around to face me, but his features are flat and unreadable.

Pushing off the bed, I stand and raise my arms. "Jesus, I can't believe you think I'd . . . what does that say about me? You think I'm some cheap skank that would drop my panties for the first loser that looks my way?" Every part of my body feels like it's been filled with wet sand, weighing me down.

Cooper blinks several times, a look of surprise on his face that pisses me off. "You didn't sleep with Kyle?"

"No. I didn't." There's a bite in my tone, and I hope he hears it. "But there's still a few hours left in the day. I'm sure I—"

Suddenly, he pulls me in, wrapping his arms around me so tight I have to fight for oxygen. "I'm sorry. You know I don't think you're a skank. I assumed he . . . I would've . . ." He pulls away, his hands gripping my shoulders, and looks into my eyes. Something unspoken settles between us but not long enough for me have a feeling about it one way or another. He briefly drops his gaze to the floor and when he looks back up, his eyes are narrowed and angry again. "You know I'd kill anyone that hurt you."

"I know, Coop," I mumble against his chest. "That's why I've been calling you non-stop. Why haven't you answered?"

He sits back down on my bed, pulling me down with him. "Shit. I dropped it in the toilet and it went code black on me. I've got it in a bag of rice."

I frown and have to think about it for a second. "How did you . . . why were you holding your phone while . . . eww, never mind." I punch his leg to relieve some of my frustrated anger, but it doesn't help enough to stop wishing genital warts on Roxanna. "If you feel duped out of pounding someone into the ground, you could always take a swing at Roxanna Talbot. Or hold her legs while I kick her ass."

Cooper laughs so hard, the bed shakes, which makes me laugh. It feels good to switch emotions. Anger is like a cancer that eats little pieces of me, and I can feel my personality morphing into something ugly.

"You want me to hold her legs," his voice rises an octave as he makes fun of me, "while you slap her with these sweet little girl arms." He gives my biceps a squeeze, proving to the both of us that I have zero muscle, and possibly no bones either.

I smirk and narrow my eyes at him. "You're an ass, Cooper Sterling."

"Maybe, but you know you're lucky to have me." He flashes that cocky smile that used to drive me insane. It has a different affect on me today but I school the tiny niggle in my chest, and decide to save the interpretation for another day.

"Damn straight." I send an elbow into his thigh and summons my smart ass. "Luckiest girl in the world to have this large lummox on my side."

He gives my knee a squeeze until I squeal and stands to leave. The laughter slowly fades and I can see relief wash over him. "I'm glad it was just a rumor, B. You deserve better." There's something in his voice that I can't discern. "Someone who loves you and knows how to treat you right." He walks to the door and stops to look back. "As far as Roxanna, ignore her. She's a jealous bitch that just got dumped by her high school sweetheart. I think he's with her best friend now. Watch and see, she'll self-destruct all on her own."

Geez. I fold my arms over my chest. "Well, now I feel sorry for her. Thanks a lot."

He smirks. "I do what I can to keep the asshole rep alive." He tips his head before stepping through the door, only his face peeking around the door frame now. "One-four-three."

Before I can say it back, he's gone. It's something we've said since we were kids. Our version of I love you. I can hear six-year old Cooper in my head, *"Without all the squishy romantic shit."* We thought we were cool having a code that no one knew about. I still whisper it into the empty room, for my sake and as a thank you for having a best friend like him. Someone that has my back no matter what. I know he would've been disappointed if the rumor were true, but not in me. He'd be disappointed that I got duped. That I had an experience that wasn't worthy of my expectations. Cooper Sterling was the best thing I had going for myself, and it was my mission to make sure he knew it.

One-four-three, Coop.

CHAPTER *two*

Cooper

It's two in the morning when I finally fall asleep on the hard surface of my Business Communications textbook. I have no doubt I'm drooling on the pages, but I can't move my head the five inches onto my pillow. My body is too drained from studying for exams and worrying about Briley. The thought of someone hurting her, taking her body without permission, physically causes me pain.

There are so many levels to our relationship, always changing and morphing into something new. We have a strong connection. Stronger than anything I've ever felt with my own sister. Maybe because she's older and never needed me the way Briley has.

It's strange though, I've always felt the need to protect her like she was my little sister, but I'm attracted to her—unlike a sister—and have to hide that fact because we're best friends and have been since we were kids. I tried to tell her once, in fifth grade. Big mistake. It made things uncomfortable between us for a long time, and I thought I'd lost her friendship for good.

But girls are fickle, and I guess she changed her mind about hanging out with me again. So I keep my feelings to myself. I try—and fail—not to be overprotective, and treat her like one of the guys. If she didn't have the longest lashes I've ever seen, surrounding those large brown orbs of innocence, and the sexiest curves every guy dreams about, I could easily treat her like one of the dudes. She can even hold her own on the basketball court and smack talk with the best of them. *Fucking sexy as hell.*

On the outside I'm holding up pretty well, living college life to the fullest. I've got girls, a pretty fair course load—my earliest class is ten a.m.—and a group of buddies that like to hang out on the weekends and strum out a few chords. But I crave more. Every night I fall asleep alone. And every night I dream of Briley.

The sound of my bedroom door creaking wakes me up, but I'm only able to mumble around my fatigue. When the creaking continues, I get the sick feeling I'm about to get punked. I'm all about a good prank and having fun, but not tonight, not now.

Feeling around, I find my pillow and pull it over my head. "Fuck off," I mumble, raising my arm to flip off the disturber of my slumber.

"Sorry, sorry," her small, sweet voice whispers before the door begins to close.

"Briley?" I roll over, pull the pillow away from my eyes, and squint to focus. "Come in." I wave my hand until she steps through the door. "What's going on?" It's not out of the norm for her to come over unannounced, but it's late. "What time is it?" Maybe it's early, and I slept past my alarm.

"Sorry, Coop." I can hear the regret in her voice. "It's really late. I shouldn't have come. Go back to sleep." She turns to leave.

"B—" I throw back the covers and fling my legs over the side of the bed. "C'mere." My arm stretches out to her, staying suspended in the air until she reaches the bed and takes a seat next to me.

"I thought you'd still be awake." She rolls her head back and sighs. "Actually, I didn't consider it. I planned to sneak in."

"You okay?" My eyes have finally adjusted, and there's enough moonlight filtering through the window to see she's been crying.

"Yeah, just a rotten day, you know?" Her hands are in her lap and she's fidgeting, pushing her cuticles back like she always does when she's about to cry. It's a distraction for her.

I wrap an arm around her and pull her into my side, her head automatically resting on my arm. Growing up next door to each other, there were many nights when she climbed through my bedroom window and curled up next to me in bed. I learned a long time ago not to try and fix her, but to listen and just be there. She used to cry about her father's death a lot, and that's not something anyone can fix. Sometimes people just need to grieve, and the only thing they want is the warmth and comfort of someone they trust to release those precious tears with.

But this isn't about her dad tonight. This is about the rumor. My instinct is to fix it, but I don't know how. If it was

19

a dude, I'd kick his ass, but a girl spread these rumors so I'm at a loss.

"Did something else happen? You said you confronted her and said what needed to—"

"Nothing else happened," she interrupts me. "I just can't believe anyone can be so vicious." Her body stiffens before she scoots around to face me. "Who raises these types of people? I mean . . . shit. Why does she hate me so much?" She's getting heated, her whisper getting louder. "Better yet, why the hell does she care so much about my sex life? Does she expect me to check in with her?" She's in full animated speech mode, one arm in the air, the other hand next to her ear like she's holding a phone. "Hello, Roxanna. What can I do today to please your fancy ass?"

A light chuckle slips out. "You don't care what she thinks—"

"No, I don't." A balled fist rests on her hip while she snaps out, "Hooker."

"Cheap hooker," I second her. "Probably only gets five bucks for head."

"Gross," she protests, wrinkling her cute little nose. "Too far, Coop." She laughs and I feel I've done my part. I love to hear her intoxicating giggle. She can't do it without it lighting up her entire face, and when she laughs, you join her.

A long moment of silence follows. It's not uncomfortable, though. Nothing's ever been uncomfortable with her. Except the cold shoulder in fifth grade, of course, but that was a long time ago.

Without saying a word, I lie back on my pillow and pull her down with me, easing the comforter over us. She assumes the position—her head on my chest, one arm draped over my stomach—and we fall asleep.

I still dream about her. Always do.

***

Exams are finally over, and I don't think I've ever been so grateful for the break. Everything I need for the next month is packed, and I've shoved every piece of clothing I own into a couple of garbage bags to wash. You don't realize how bad things smell until you pile them together in one place. Like the odor's been amplified.

It didn't work out for Briley and me to drive home together. Her exams ended before mine, and she was eager to get home. Which is fine. I need the time alone. Christmas is her favorite holiday, so I take the entire drive home to think of what to get her.

Two and half hours later, when I open the front door to my childhood home, the scent of Christmas welcomes me. Mix the comfort of being in your childhood home with the scent of cinnamon and bottled pine trees and there's no feeling to top it.

After the ceremonial hugs and catch up conversation with Mom, Dad, and my sister, Claire, I start a load of laundry before my mom can get hold of it. She wouldn't complain about washing my clothes, but she'd give me an earful of how bad everything smells and ask me why I wasn't using the apartment laundry room. Then I'd have to make some shit up about how it's broken or nasty. But the truth is, I'm lazy.

***

I haven't seen Briley in almost two weeks and it's killing me. We've been reduced to texting and short phone calls between holiday parties and shopping. I'm having dinner with her and her mom tonight—Christmas Eve, per our yearly tradition. They always come to a party at our house on New Year's Eve, but I have to break the news to her tonight that I won't be there this year.

My parents and sister are in the living room when I'm ready to head out. They're watching *It's a Wonderful Life* like they do every year. I love the traditions my family keeps.

"I'm going over," I announce.

"You're not wearing a tie?" My mother starts to get up, but I hold up a hand.

"No. I'm wearing a button down. Good enough." I've got on a white shirt that I've ironed and a clean pair of jeans. I feel pretty good about the way I've cleaned up. But even though I'm twenty years old, I have no doubt my mother would stick a tie around my neck and tuck my hair behind my ears if I let her.

Claire wiggles her eyebrows up and down, slipping into the annoying big sister role. "Have fun."

I give her the finger, but we're both smiling.

"Don't forget the packages," Dad calls out over his shoulder. "And tell Briley and Nina Merry Christmas for us."

"Will do." I nod and step outside into the cool air.

Ten steps and I'm at the front door, pressing the red nose on the reindeer doorbell Briley's mom puts out every year.

The door swings open and Briley nearly knocks me off the front porch when she jumps into my arms. "Merry Christmas, Coop!" Her welcome is so animated, you'd think we haven't seen each other in months.

I can't help my sarcasm. "It's so good to finally see you, B. You've changed so much over the past two weeks."

A punch to the arm is delivered as expected. "Shut up," she says. Her goofy grin makes me smile. "You know this is my favorite holiday."

Every year I get a tour of the house so I can see the decorations Briley and her mom worked so hard on. My family puts up a tree, and we decorate the hell out of it with every ornament my parents have collected over the years. But the Sheffield's house is Christmas on crack.

Briley takes my hand and leads me through their own personal Christmas village. The living room hosts a traditional tree with every handmade ornament Briley has ever made from preschool up, plus an ornament from every vacation spot they've ever been to. She has a white tree in her bedroom with Hello Kitty ornaments. (Yeah, she still hasn't outgrown the kitty, and I wonder if she ever will.) The guest bathroom has a miniature tree that sits on the countertop. It has cream and gold balls, matching the bathroom décor. The dining room tree is done in crosses of every shape, size, and color, her mother's favorite. And finally, the one in the kitchen is dressed in kitchen type stuff—tiny whisks and measuring cups. I only know this because she has shown me the same trees every year.

Instead of studying the decorations, I watch Briley's expression as she tells me about them. She's so happy and excited that I soak her up and feed off her energy like a battery charge.

"What the hell is this?" I ask, lifting a gold porcelain boot and letting it fall back down. The creature looks part elf, part old lady, with a touch of Santa.

"It's Mr. Claus, of course." Her face pinches as she looks at me like I've lost my head.

"I don't think so, B. You've been duped. This . . . thing looks nothing like—"

"Gah!" She rolls her eyes and picks up the porcelain doll. "It's art, Coop."

Oh. Art. What the hell was I thinking? "It's weird."

"I agree." She shrugs a shoulder and huffs out a sweet giggle.

The wonderful smells coming from the kitchen are a welcome distraction. My stomach growls just as Mrs. Sheffield calls us to the dining room.

Briley picks at her dinner while I clean my plate. Mrs. Sheffield is a magnificent cook and I've stuffed myself on ham, turkey, sweet potatoes, and her homemade flaky rolls until I'm uncomfortable. I have to pass on dessert until after we open presents. I can't wait to see Briley's reaction to my gift. She's going to flip, I'm sure of it.

Briley's mom waves me off when I try to help clear the table. "You two go on. I'm going to have a cup of coffee and leave the dishes for a bit."

Briley bounces into the living room, and I follow behind. I take a seat on the floor, leaning against the base of the couch. We do this every year and I have to check myself so she doesn't see through me. Truth is, I love being with her during the holidays. The way her eyes light up over every detail—food, decorating, presents, she even loves wrapping presents. This right here, being with her, feels like home as much as my own home does.

"Open mine first." Briley shoves a box into my lap and plops herself down next to me. The package is wrapped in red and green plaid paper with an intricate red bow on top. I'm careful not to tear into it, purposefully moving slow to torment her. She's always been impatient, tearing into her packages, and it drives her nuts when others don't do the same. With a groan she reaches across my lap and jerks the bow off in one swift motion. "Hurry up, grandma."

"I thought I'd iron the paper and reuse it next year," I joke. "Don't rush me." I plant my elbow into her side and give her a gentle push before tearing into the paper and lifting the lid off the box. I'm eager to see what's inside, because she gets me and always delivers the perfect gift. I know her, too, but I'm a terrible gift giver. Except this year. Nailed it.

Inside the box is a stack of vinyl records and I stare at them for a moment. I started collecting vinyl last year and had a list of ones I really wanted to find but couldn't. But here they all were. *How?* "Where did you find these?" I flip through and see Lynard Skynyrd, The Beetles, and The Eagles. "These are all on my list."

"I know." She shrugs a shoulder like it's no big deal. "I've got stealthy moves, Coop. You should know that by now."

"Yeah, yeah," I chuckle. "The CIA will be recruiting you any day now." My head shakes in disbelief, the smile on my lips refusing to retreat. For the second time, I flip each album over, studying the back and front. I know how hard it must have been for her to find these and I'm touched. If I didn't have a mad crush on her, I might even get choked up. I steal a glance in her direction. Her hands are clasped under her chin while a wide smile is stretches across her sweet lips. Those eyes—dark brown orbs that cast wicked spells on me. I wonder when things will change between us. I know she'll be mine one day, I just need her to figure it out and get on board.

My thoughts are interrupted when she rests her head on my shoulder. "This is my favorite part of Christmas."

"Which part?"

She takes a deep breath and exhales a relaxed sigh. "Watching your expression when you have something you love."

I'm taken aback and I feel my body stiffen, wondering if she's finally getting it. *It's you. You have to feel it. You must know?* I want to take her by the shoulders, look into her eyes, and tell her, but it didn't work out too well for me last time. Instead, I lean my head over to rest on hers. "Thanks, B. Perfect gift."

She tucks a long strand of her dark brown hair behind her ear and rubs her hands together. "Okay, now where's mine?" She springs to her feet and hops over to the packages I set down when I arrived.

I just laugh because she's so damn adorable. "The small one's for your mom."

Her eyes light up, but I'm sure they would over either package. Carrying the bigger package over, she sits down next to me and looks it over. Now she decides to be patient?

"Sorry, bum wrap job." I shrug, not sure why I'm stating the obvious. I've never liked the process of wrapping.

"It looks great." She pulls on the tape and rips into the paper. "Got a little excited with the tape, didn't you?" Inside is a large stocking, bulky with the goodies I've filled it with, and her name glitter-glued to the front. "Did you craft for me?" she drawls and adds a smirk.

"Hell no. I've still got my man card." My eyebrows knit together and I lean away from her insult. "One of Ryan's girlfriend's did it for me." As soon as the words leave my lips, I know it sounds shitty and hope she isn't offended by a random girl helping with her present. I try to recover. "I picked out the stocking, though. All she did was write your name for me. Wait 'til you see what's inside."

Briley lifts the stocking out of the box, sets it in her lap, and tosses the box aside. "What's in here?"

I shrug, feeling like the delivery guy on *Christmas Vacation*. "Open it up and see."

Stockings have always been her absolute favorite part of Christmas. I don't get it, but she gets silly excited about hand lotions and nail polish when they're stuffed in her monogrammed stocking over the fireplace. So I combined her gift and stocking this year, purposefully layering the items for her to pull out. On the top I put chapstick and candies, in the middle are things like lotions and gift cards, and the main gift is on the bottom.

"This is so exciting." She wiggles, pulling each item out like it's the finest gift she's ever received. "You can paint my toes," she informs me, grinning mischievously as she holds up the bottle of blue polish.

I make a face. "I don't think that would be fun for either of us." A man has to draw the line at polish.

With a laugh, she pulls out the next item, a movie theater gift card. "Ooh, I've been dying to see that space movie. What's it called?" Tossing it aside, she immediately yanks out the next gift card. "Ah, we can go to dinner first, then the movies." Her eyes get even wider with excitement.

I give her a warm smile and push her hair behind her shoulder so I can see her face. "You don't have to take me. These things are for you."

"Who else would I want to go with?" She looks at me like I've grown another set of eyeballs and keeps digging through the stocking until she pulls out one of the main gifts. I'm nervous, hoping she likes it. Fuck, it's fifth grade all over again.

Silence.

Her jaw is slack as she studies it, still not saying a word. Finally, her expression changes, but it looks sad. I have a gut-sinking feeling that I've missed something. I'm not sure what I've done wrong, but I want to take it out of her hands and tell her I've made a mistake, that it was meant for someone else.

"Oh my God, Coop," she whispers. "It's too much."

"Nah. It's really not," I insist, trying not to panic. "Seriously, I stayed within our limit." I'm actually setting myself up for every future Christmas, giving her this charm bracelet. Now I can add a charm every year from the places she travels or dreams of going one day. I nod toward the stocking. "There's something still in there, though. I worked really hard to get it for you. Us, actually."

She cocks her head as she looks at me, curious about what's in there or maybe about my meaning of *us*. Reaching

28

in, she feels around and pulls out the prize, taking time to read the words on the tickets.

"How did you get these? It's sold out." Her eyes are wide with disbelief, and it's totally worth the trouble I went through.

I huff out a heavy sigh. "Sold my soul to the devil. They better be worth it."

"Seriously, Coop. Foo Fighters? How?"

"A friend of a friend of a friend of Ryan's." My words spill out in an exhausted pattern as I pretend it was a really big deal. Maybe it will soften the blow of disappointment I have to deliver. "I made a few promises and paid too much for them, but I'm excited. You know I'm going with you, right?" We've loved this band forever, and since I learned to play "Everlong," she makes me break out the guitar and play it at least once a week. I'm definitely accompanying her.

"Of course you are!" she squeals.

She throws herself in my lap, arms wrapped around my neck, and I can feel every curve of her body pressed against me, including her firm tits and sweet little ass. The entire house smells like pine and fresh baked cookies—until this moment, when my nose is buried in her hair. She smells clean and happy, if that's a scent. It's the only way to describe Briley Sheffield. Beautiful, clean, and happy. But the lack of strong floral perfume isn't the only thing that separates her from all the other girls. There's something about her—always has been—that pulls me in and makes me want to be around her, friend zone or not. She's comfortable and unnerving at the same time, causing a constant state of pandemonium inside of me.

Scooting out of my lap, she adjusts her shirt, smoothing invisible wrinkles as if it would matter. There's an uncomfortable blush to her cheeks, which piques my curiosity and has my heart feeling like it's jacked up on Red Bull. Is she finally feeling something? *Please, God.*

"So, what's the devil like?" she asks, throwing me even more off balance. All I can do is stare at her, wondering if I've missed a whole conversation while taking in the smell and feel of the girl I've been crushing on for years. "You sold your soul . . . is he terrifying?" She holds her hands over her head like horns, wiggling her fingers.

We share an awkward laugh, which buys me some time to get my thoughts together. "Yeah, yeah, the horns are kinda cartoonish. It's the eyes that haunt your dreams." I squint and give her my best evil face.

She just giggles and hangs the bracelet I got her over her wrist, reaching out for me to clasp it. As I'm latching it, I tell her my news, what I've been dreading telling her all evening. "I won't be here for the New Year's Eve party. The band's been invited to play at Puckett's."

I see the clear disappointment on her face, though she tries to hide it behind a shaky smile. "Really? That's—wow, Coop, that's amazing!"

Sweet Briley. She's excited for me. It comes out in her words. But her face tells a different story. I've let her down.

CHAPTER
Three

Cooper

It's the same every night, staying up until I can't keep my eyes open, hoping I'll be too exhausted to dream of the girl I can't have. Tonight is different, though, and I fall asleep worried instead of frustrated. Briley's been in a funk, but she won't tell me why. She's not acting pissed over me ditching our annual New Year's Eve plan, but she's not spending every minute with me like we usually do, either. Normally I can read her like a book, but this time I can't. Every time I call, she texts that damn auto response, *Sorry, can't talk right now.* When she finally calls me back, she sounds neighborly and rushed.

I'll get to the bottom of it in the morning. Right now, I need sleep. Tomorrow's a big night for me and the guys, and I'm sure as hell not going to stay up all night worrying and risk ruining the event for everyone.

But just as my body relaxes and I'm taken to that glorious 'almost there' sleep state, I hear my window slide open. Briley is usually stealthy when she sneaks in. A few times I've woken up with her by my side, not even realizing she'd come in. But tonight she's purposely making sure I wake up and acknowledge her presence. She's knocked over my desk lamp, tripped on something in the floor, and her version of curse words are flying. "Garden seeds, that hurt! You live like a pig, Coop."

"B? Keep it down. Jesus!" I yell-whisper, jumping up to help her before she wakes my parents. Even though there's nothing physical between us, both of our mothers would freak if they knew she sneaks in my window. Her mom won't even let her close the door if the opposite sex is in the room. Friend zoned or not.

"Are you awake?" she asks as she falls into my arms.

"No, I've just got a badass hologram system."

She doesn't laugh at my sarcasm. I guess she's still pissed at me. "Can we talk?" She feels her way around the room until she reaches the bed and takes a seat.

"Yeah." Finally, we're going to get this shit out of the way, and I can get a peaceful night's sleep. I sit next to her on the bed, and we both start at the same time.

"Listen, B—"

"Coop, I've been thinking—"

"Go ahead." I nod in the darkness. Feeling her close to me right now stirs everything and wrecks all common sense for anything off-limits.

"It's really hot in here." She pulls off her long sleeve shirt and tosses it to the floor. I've seen Briley in her bra before. I've seen her in her bikini, which covers even less. But the sight of her sitting on my bed, a thin layer of lace the only barrier between my greedy hands and her perfect tits, makes the blood rush instantly and my boxers do nothing to help me hide it. *Fuck.*

"I'll open the window." *Why the hell couldn't we have snow, just this once?* I need to cool off before I can face her again, so I pretend to study something outside. "What were you going to say?"

She doesn't answer, but I can hear her shimmying out of her pajama pants. So much for easing my erection. I have no doubt her panties match the lace bra, and I'm sure my hard-on can't be hidden or relieved without a trip to the bathroom. I wait for what sounds like Briley climbing under the covers before I feel safe enough to turn around, trying to recite the Periodic Table of Elements as a distraction. I hated Chemistry, and it's not doing me any damn favors now either.

Briley's on her back, on her side of the bed, so I climb in and rest my hands behind my head. "I'm sorry I'm bailing on you New Year's Eve, but this is really important to us. You understand, right?"

She rolls over and rests her head on my chest, snuggling into my side. My right arm instinctively comes down, my hand ready to protect my secret boner.

"You think I'm mad?" She giggles. It's the sweetest sound, but I can also smell the liquor on her breath. "I'm so proud of you, Coopy."

Fuck, I hate that nickname. Hate. It. "How much have you had to drink, B?"

"Not much." Her fingers begin swirling imaginary designs across my chest, and it's hard not to enjoy it for a little longer, pretend we're a couple. I'm not afraid to admit why I'm afraid to tell her how I feel. The last time I laid it out, I lost her for a while. Worst year of my existence. That—though it was eons ago—is enough to last me a while.

"Hey." Rolling to my side, I face her. "What did you drink?"

"Mom made that lemonade concoction. She made a bunch." She drags the word out, giving me a good idea about just how much she drank. "Her friends are so hoity-toity. You should've seen what Mrs. Parsons was wearing." She raises her hands in the air and looks at them like she's discovering she has fingers for the first time. "I filled a CamelBak before hiding in my room to get away from them." *That's my Briley.* I smirk in the darkness, shaking my head at the thought of her sitting in her room, drinking from her U of F Gators CamelBak. That's a fucking huge container.

I have to sit up to get my head around how much she drank. I know too well about this lemonade concoction. It's delicious and you have no idea you've drank too much until you've actually had too much. Who thought to mix vodka and champagne together and make it taste like a sweet, summer refresher?

No doubt she's staying here tonight so I can watch over her. I also have no doubt about the sleep deprivation I'll feel for tomorrow night's gig. Hopefully I can sneak in a nap.

Briley sits up and snuggles into me again. I love the way it feels, the way she feels, but I also have a feeling she's about to puke at any time. Before I settle in, I hop off the bed and grab my trash can, just in case, placing it next to my bed before climbing back in. Now I know the secret to getting rid of a hard-on—think about vomit. "How're you feeling?"

"I feel amazing." She stretches her arms overhead before wrapping herself around me again. "You good?"

I nod, even though she probably doesn't see it. "Think you can sleep? Do you feel sick?"

"I'm fine." She doesn't sound fine; she sounds like she could go clubbing for the next four hours, and I prepare myself for her talkative side.

Easing myself down, I pull up the comforter and cover us both. Just when I'm ready for her to take her spot, settled into my side, she props herself up on an elbow. "Do you think I'm pretty?"

The question floors me. It's so unexpected.

Briley exhales a heavy, disappointed sigh, and I barely make out what she whispers to herself. "Maybe Kyle Greer is the one for me after all."

Fuck-to-the-no for Kyle Greer! What does that douchebag have to do with anything? "Of course I think you're pretty, B. What the hell kind of question is that? You know you're gorgeous." My voice is clipped, and I regret the way it comes off as irritated and impatient.

"No, *you* know you're gorgeous, Coop." She sits up again, and I wonder if I'll be the first to get motion sickness even though I'm sober. "You've got girls following you around, throwing their panties at your feet. I've got a stupid rumor and my goddamn virginity."

Before I can answer, her lips crash into mine. It's clumsy and desperate, but it feels like the best kiss I've ever had because they're Briley's lips.

"B," I manage as I force myself to pull back. My lips immediately miss hers. "That's bullshit and you know it." I have too much to say, yet I'm speechless at the same time. All I can think about is kissing her, but she needs to know why I'm kissing her, why I want her. Not because she's some girl, present in my room. But because she's . . . everything.

"We've never lied to each other, Coop." Her voice is quiet, filled with unhappiness, and she's pushing on her cuticles. "Please, best friends honor, tell me the truth now. What am I doing wrong?"

I'm in a state of panic as I watch the sadness on her face taking her down faster than I can pull her back up. At the same time I notice her lace-covered tits heaving with each breath. Taking my gaze off of them, I glance down only to see her flat stomach, the deep curve of her waist, and the hem of her lace panties resting against smooth flesh. Untouched flesh, which for some reason makes me want her more. To know that I could be the only man that ever touches her, would ever touch her, makes me realize I could easily give up every woman on the planet and be only hers.

Her shoulders shake once, bringing me back to reality. Tears pool and cling to her lashes.

Tucking my hand under her chin, I pull her closer to me, less than a whisper's distance. "You're the most beautiful woman I've ever laid eyes on," I begin. As each truth leaves my mouth, it's as if a constricting vine has been clipped, freeing parts of me. "Smart, sexy, funny . . . and you're doing everything right." She blinks a few times and a tear travels down her cheek. By the look on her face, she's not convinced. "Do you hear me? Everything right."

"Coop." My name is a statement, not a question when it leaves her lips. The one syllable word tells me everything I've longed to hear, and I take the luxury of elaborating on the unspoken. Together, we lean in closer. Although I know it's coming, nothing prepares me for the intensity of our first kiss. As close as we are, it seems an eternity before our lips meet. When they do, we completely fuse together. She tastes like sweet Florida ripened lemons and pure sunshine. For a fleeting moment I remember that she drank a shit ton of that lemon concoction, but then her arm snakes around the back of my neck and I'm caught up in the tantalizing flames licking taking over all thought and reason.

My hand comes up to rest on the smooth flesh just above her hip and I tug her closer. Her kiss is still soft, yet powerful enough to erase all memories of other kisses. She's the one. She's always been the one. My heart has known this truth since fifth grade. My body, well, since . . . damn, her little whimpers are so distracting. I've wanted this moment most of my life and now that it's here my heart and flesh are battling. My heart says, *Take it slow, fucker, don't screw this up. Go for it.* But my body screams, *She wants you, you want her. Don't fuck this up.*

Briley's sweet voice, laced with need, barges through the battle front and demands every ounce of my attention. "Cooper, I want you."

Palms slide over skin, moans vibrate off of tongues, and any control I had over my body, thoughts and feelings are lost. *Cooper, I want you* plays on repeat. I'm a paralyzed fool, letting the act of falling in love take over my entire being.

"I want you, too," I breathe. *Always have.* When Briley moves to straddle my lap, I push off the headboard to lean into her. The softness of our first kiss has passed and is replaced with a hunger so fucking deep, it's like an uncaged animal inside my chest. I can't think of anything else besides touching her, and I want everything all at once. My hands cup her face to bring her in closer, then slide down her long neck and onto her shoulders. The sexiest moan leaves her mouth, nearly making me lose my shit as Briley encourages me to move further. It's the permission I need to let my hand skim down her side, my fingers teasing the lace of her bra before traveling to the dip of her waist. She presses her chest into mine, lifting her ass slightly as my hands reach around to cup the firmness. The way we move together is perfection, the timing flawless.

I know without a fucking doubt that I could never get tired of kissing her. The feelings that wash over me when we're together like this is indescribable and nothing I've ever felt with another girl. I want to go slow, not rush, savor everything, but the greedy bastard inside of me still wants more. I crave her taste and want to cover every inch of her sweetness. Dipping my head, I nip at her ear and kiss my way along her jawline and throat. It only takes a second to unclasp her bra and get my hands on her tits, then I'm reminded of her question earlier and bite back a laugh. *"Do you think I'm pretty?"* She's fucking perfect. So much so that I'm overcome with an animalistic need to tear the room apart so I don't take my sexual aggression out on her.

To ease the beast, I take a deep breath. I have to save a piece of my mind from falling under this spell and remember to be gentle with her. She's never done this before, and I love her too much to hurt her. Mustering every ounce of tenderness, I lift her off my lap, ease her back on the bed, and hover over her as I untangle her bra from her arms and toss it to the floor. I have to steal a moment to take in the sight of her. Her long dark hair is sprawled against my grey sheets, while her large brown orbs of lust look at me with trust and want. She's killing me.

I'm a cliché, a laughable pussy in this moment. "I love you, Briley Sheffield. You're beautiful and perfect." As soon as the words come out of my mouth, I feel like I've said too much, wrecked the moment.

But then she pulls back the bow that releases an arrow to my heart. I love you, too, Coop." The words I've longed to hear leave her mouth and I take a moment to savor them. Her eyes don't paint the same picture I imagine of someone in love though. They're playful, not serious and loving like I expected. "Thank you for doing this for me . . . being my first."

Suddenly, it feels like someone has punched me in the stomach, and I can't breathe or think straight. That's why she wants this? I'm doing her a favor, taking her virginity like it's a bad virus? I lean back on my heels, studying her from my now sobered eyes. "What's wrong?" She sits up, crossing her arms over her chest like she's just now realizing she's topless.

My eyes squeeze shut against her perfect, almost naked body so I can take back control. "I shouldn't have let it go this far." My head won't stop shaking as all the reasons I'm a dick for letting this much happen come flooding in. She's drunk. She doesn't love me the way I love her. She trusts me not to take advantage of her and that's what I'm doing. "You're drunk."

"I want this, Coop." She reaches her hand around the back of my head and pulls herself to her knees so we're face to face. "Please." She looks down then back up, and when our eyes lock she's hooked me again. "Please." Her lips press against mine, her tongue sliding in to find mine in an erotic dance that I can't refuse. She grips my dick, a little more aggressive than is comfortable, and I'm stone hard again in an instant.

Fuck. Fuck, fuck!

I know she's had too much to drink, I'm certain she'll regret it in the morning, and I just now realize I've left the box of condoms in my apartment at school. *Goddammit.* I had no reason to have them here. It's a sign for sure and I make a promise to myself, Briley, and God on the spot that I will not take her tonight. We can't risk it. And I'd be a douche for taking advantage of her in this state. I repeat it once more in my head so it's sculpted in my brain matter. *Can't risk it.* But as she reaches in my boxers and strokes my length, softly but with a boldness as if it belongs to her alone. My resolve melts, and a grin precedes a groan as I think of all the things we can do without going all the way.

Like a bee to pollen, my right hand that's resting on her hip travels to her tiny cotton shorts, pushing them down until I feel the lace of her panties. Her body tenses so I still, but then she groans and pushes her hip into my hand.

Ever so slowly I dip lower until I meet the warmth that I so desperately want but refuse to claim tonight. It's obvious she's turned on, and I love that it's because of me. When I feel how wet she is I almost come undone like a teen that's just hit puberty. Inhaling is no longer a need for oxygen; it's to breathe each other in. Exhales turn to panting; Whimpers fuel the fire brewing inside both of us to a dangerous level. We find a rhythm stroking each other. I'm holding on with every bit of strength and have to stop her once for a break.

Her breathing is erratic and she's gripping the back of my neck so tightly I'm sure she's about to tip over the edge. And I haven't even touched her flesh yet. I want more, so I slip my hand inside her panties. She's smooth, soft, and so intoxicating. *Fuck.* I've never wanted anything as much as I want her. Every sense is magnified, pulling for more. The sight of her back arching as my fingers stroke her, a vanilla and Ivory soap clean that belongs only to her, the taste of her lemon infused lips calling me to taste every inch of her, the way she feels in my arms, is all too much.

Fuck me.

She's pulling at my boxers, and if it was any other night I wouldn't hesitate. But I love her too much to take her like this, drunk off her ass on the lemon punch. If she had made her feelings known even yesterday, I might be convinced that this was okay.

My body wants her, my heart wants her, but my mind wins in the end and I can't take advantage.

"Stop," I choke out, then lean back, regretfully pulling her hand out of my boxers. My body screams in protest, but this is the way it has to be. "If we don't stop now, I won't be able to."

"Exactly." She giggles as she reaches for me again, but I force myself to roll off the bed and pull on a pair of shorts. *Where's the damn armor when you need it?* Her shoulders slump and I can physically see the defeat on her face as her inner demons tell her she's not wanted.

Rubbing the back of my neck, I let out a disappointed sigh. "I want you, B, believe me I do." I'm on the bed, facing her in an instant, picking up her lifeless hands in mine. She has to know why I can't take this further. "But not when you're drunk like this. And I don't have—"

"I'm not drunk, asshole." Her words slam into me like a sledgehammer. She's hurt, angry, maybe embarrassed. I can't read her when she's like this. The defeat is gone as she collects her things. I reach for her waist, but she twists away and goes to the window.

"Bri, listen," I start, but I have no idea what to say to her. My entire body is against me right now, and my brain refuses to help me out. *Stupid motherfucker.*

Briley scoops up her shoes and bra, tucking them under her arm. "I just needed . . . why couldn't you . . . shit, Coop, let's just forget this happened." Her voice is thick with anger but I see the hurt in her eyes and I so desperately want to fix this. *Think!* The words sound stupid in my head and refuse to leave my mouth. *I don't have condoms or I totally would've . . .* Stupid. *Let's try again tomorrow, when . . .* I'm not even the drunk one and I sound like a fool.

She raises my window, not caring about all the noise she's making as she starts to climb through. "Shit," she repeats as she stumbles through the window and falls to the ground.

I climb out behind her to make sure she makes it home. Not drunk, my ass. The way she's walking confirms she's had too much to drink. Once she's safely inside her bedroom window, I take my time, enjoying the crisp air biting into my bare chest. I need to clear my mind, wrap my brain around what just happened. *Didn't happen.*

Feeling like a total asshole, I lift my head and whisper to Mother Nature, "I could really use some fucking snow in this damn town."

CHAPTER four

Cooper

The next morning, I'm able to sleep until noon, thank God. The house is quiet when I get up and, after turning on the Keurig, I see the note from Ma.

Gone to lunch. Knew you'd rather sleep. Text if you want us to bring you something home.

All I want is coffee, Motrin, and to know Briley's okay. She hasn't called or texted today, so I click on her number. It goes to voicemail. Instead of leaving a lame message, stumbling over words and sounding like an ass, I type out a text, which I edit several times.

Hey

Yes, that brilliance took me several attempts. But Briley knows me. She knows that hey means, *How are you feeling this morning? Any regrets? Did we go too far? Are you still pissed or are we good?*

What can I say, I'm a man. We don't do a lot of words.

When I don't hear back from her, I decide to get a little more creative.

You okay?

An hour later she responds.

I'm fine.

The timing is terrible since the guys just got here and we're all set up to rehearse for tonight. I don't have time to actually talk to her on the phone. *Fantastic.*

Me: Will I see you today?

Briley: I'm out with my mom all day.

And that's it. I can feel her separating herself from me. She's either still embarrassed or hurt or disgusted that she crossed the line with me. I hope it's not the latter. I don't know how to fix this, but I can't worry about it right now. The guys are already giving me shit about being on the phone.

Me: I'll talk to you later, OK? Rehearsing. 1-4-3

Typing the last three digits makes me feel like a pussy, but she's worth it. We've never left a conversation without saying our version of I love you and I need her to know, especially now, that I do love her, even if it's our childhood version.

She responds, **OK.** With a period at the end. No numbers.

I'm dumbfounded, heartsick, and pissed at the same time. Girls are the most ridiculously complicated beings on earth.

I glance up at my band mate who's giving me an impatient glare. "Ryan, if a girl responded to a text with 'OK' and put a period at the end, what would that mean to you?"

Ryan taps his drumsticks against the sides of his legs and shakes his head. "She's pissed." He smirks. "What did your dumbass do this time?"

I shake him off and start playing the first chords of our opening song. "We need to work on this one a few more times and are we playing New Year's Day by U2?"

"We have to," Gavin says. "It's an easy one to play."

44

With the topic of Briley off the table, we rehearse. I'm off, missing notes and forgetting an occasional lyric.

"Dude," Ryan stops playing and tosses a stick at my head. "What the fuck is up?"

A shrug of the shoulder is my only response. I can't let the guys know how bent out of shape I am over Briley. They already give me hell about her. I pull a Rolling Rock out of the mini fridge, pop the top, and take a long pull of the crisp beer. "All set." I nod and slip the strap of my guitar over my head. If only it was that easy, I'd buy a case and consume it immediately.

We rehearse for the next three hours and I'm playing like shit. I make promises to pull my head out of my ass as we all leave rehearsal. A lame excuse gets me out the door unscathed; something about a hangover and needing a shower and carbs.

The entire time I'm getting ready, all I can think about is Briley and hope this night goes by quickly. It'll be too late to see her when I get home, but I plan on slipping through her window and spending the night beside her. If she's truly pissed enough to wake up and try to kick me out, at least I'll know and we can talk it out. We've never played games with each other or been able to go through with the silent treatment, so I know we'll work it out. Until then, this night will be hell.

CHAPTER *five*

Briley

My mother won't ease up on me about not going to the Sterling house for the annual New Year's Eve party. Even when I explain that Cooper won't be there, nor anyone else my age. So I do what any nineteen-year-old would do—I lie.

"What about Claire? She'll be there."

"I have a date," I say flippantly. "I've already agreed and I can't back out."

She raises a questioning eyebrow. "Who? Do I know him?" I can see she doesn't buy my story, so I think of the one person who would never let me down. Parker Travis. I've been putting him off since last summer, lacking the courage to tell him I'm not interested. It's a problem, I know, but I've never been able to say no. I don't like to hurt people's feelings. That's one of the reasons we've switched phone companies twice and why we have three orders of thin mints from three different Girl Scouts every year.

"You know him." I shove my hands in my pockets to keep from fidgeting and giving myself away. "Parker."

"He's been after you for years. I thought you didn't like him." Her forehead wrinkles with suspicion.

One year, not years. It takes all my concentration not to roll my eyes. She hates that more than anything. "He grew up. I guess the working world has changed him." I shrug a shoulder and concentrate on a loose thread in my pocket. "Anyway, I thought I'd give him a shot. He's taking me to watch Cooper and his band play tonight."

My mother studies me for a moment before giving in. "That sounds nice. I'm sure Cooper will appreciate you being there. He and Parker get along?" She knows how protective Cooper is, that's the only reason she's letting me go to a bar on New Year's Eve.

I'm nodding my head too much when I answer, "Yeah. Cooper likes him well enough." What I really need to do is get my butt in my room and give Parker a call. Hopefully he doesn't have plans. Now that I've dug this hole, I need to make sure it plays out.

***

As we step inside Puckett's, the back of my hand is stamped with a red design, letting the bartender know not to serve me. Parker has a black stamp and heads to the bar immediately. He returns with a red solo cup that I take, draining the contents steadily as I watch Cooper flirt with the entire front row of tables. He's playing one of my favorite songs, but he's added an edge to it making it angsty. No, it's angry. I'm glad he's angry and hope he's suffering as much as I am. Why the hell did I have to get drunk and throw myself at him like that? He thinks I'm naïve, which pisses me off but I can handle it. Rejection, though, is a different story. It changes things, eats away a friendship like battery acid. *Stupid lemonade punch.*

After a long moment, I realize Cooper's watching me with narrowed eyes, his brows pulled together. Now he's looking at the drink in my hand and only I can see the slight shake of his head, telling me to get rid of it. Nothing makes me feel as stupid as when he plays the big brother act. We both know he's going to go home with some random girl tonight, but I can't even have a beer with the opposite sex.

Screw that. Pun intended.

When Parker's arm slides around my waist, I fight the urge to flinch. I know one look from me would have Cooper jumping off the manmade platform, pushing through the crowd, and wrecking the arm that's pulling me closer to Parker's side. *Whatever.* He has no say in the matter. Just because he doesn't want me, doesn't mean someone else doesn't. Parker's not that bad to look at. He's a little taller than me with curly dark hair and . . . eyes. I can't remember what color they are, but I'm sure they're just fine. His hand rests on my hip, and I decide that's acceptable. It's our first date, so I'm a little annoyed that he feels comfortable enough to touch me, but I'm numb from the rejection still brewing through me from last night. Cooper and I have been through shit before, but this feels like the worst thing for sure. I wish I could calm the storm inside, figure out why I feel so wretched. Embarrassment, shame, and anger all swirl through me, along with something else. Do I have feelings for him? Maybe I like-like him, as Ava suggested. The suck of it all is, he doesn't feel the same.

Cooper's eyes haven't left mine, and it feels way too good to have his attention on me rather than on the two girls I've aptly named Bubblegum-Lips and Denim-Painted-Legs. It's not fair to play Parker as an innocent pawn in this game, but I'm all in and it's too late. After the song ends, I can see it in Cooper's eyes as he announces that they're taking a short break. Time's up. He's coming our way.

"Parker," I smile, turning on the necessary flirt mode to get things moving. I turn the cup upside down to show it's empty. "Another?"

He grins, happy to fill me with more liquor, and walks away just in time. "I'll be right back."

When Cooper steps in front of me, he's out of breath and his grey T-shirt is dotted with sweat. His green eyes are intense as he stares me down. I know he's going for serious, but what he's giving is a sexy vibe that makes me uncomfortable in his presence. He really is gorgeous. I can see why the girls are crazy for him.

"What're you doing here?" His words grate out through clenched teeth.

"I was invited," I bite back. My fists ball up and rest on my hips at the same time one leg juts out in defense. *Your douchestache needs a razor-sharp trim.* I want to say it aloud but don't.

"By Parker-shithead-Travis?" He's so close to my face, I have to step back, which is a weakness, and it pisses me off.

"Don't get mad at him," I spit out, my index finger planted firmly on his chest. "*You* should've invited me."

He gives a curt nod. "You're right, it's just that tonight—"

"I get it," I interrupt. Although I don't get it. At all. But I know all too well Cooper's temper, and I don't want Parker to get his ass kicked tonight. I also don't want to ruin Cooper's performance. I might be hurt by his rejection, but

I'd never hurt him back, not like that. I'm proud of him and want him and his band mates to do well. "He's been a perfect gentleman, Coop. No need to worry about me tonight." It's a good idea to change the subject, ease the mood before Parker gets back and all hell breaks loose. I'm still angry with him for pushing me away. True, I drank too much, and I remember I was the one that threw myself at him. But I also remember his easy ability to say no thank you and shove me out of his window. Then, to add fuel to the fire, he doesn't invite me to watch him play. What the hell is going on with him and why isn't he honest with me anymore?

"I'm sure he is." Cooper rolls his eyes.

I sigh and decide to put my feelings on hold, make sure this night is about him. "You're playing great tonight. Enjoy yourself and don't worry about me." My fists relax and I rub Cooper's arm, immediately wishing I hadn't as my hand glides across the slippery sweat. Ten percent eww and ninety percent hot as hell. "Everyone loves you. Especially the girls." The last bit slips out in a puddle of woe-is-me, and to make it worse, I nod my head in the direction of Barbie and her sidekick.

Cooper glances at the girls and shakes his head like he's just viewed something grotesque. *Nice try, slick.*

"Tonight feels good, you know. Like a taste of what could be." He smiles and I can see in his eyes that's he's daydreaming of a future as a rock star. It suits him but saddens me because I know I'd hardly see him.

I give him a small smirk, though I sense the sorrow underneath it. "Don't forget your best friend when you're famous." A look passes between us, heavy with uncertainty, laced with distress. The moment is getting depressing and that's not how I wanted to end the year or start the new one, so I puff out a laugh and bump him with my hip. "Or I'll tell the tabloids all the goods."

Coop socks me lightly on the arm, then quickly rubs it out as if it won't count. "One, I'll never be famous. Two, Briley Sheffield forgettable? Nah, never." Cooper shakes his head and lowers his eyes before I can process the look he just blasted me with.

Not forgettable, but not fuckable either. I suck my bottom lip in and give it a bite so I won't say what I'm thinking.

When Parker returns with two drinks, my body tenses, wondering what Cooper will do or say. I can tell Parker is nervous when he doesn't hand me the drink. He's no match for Cooper, in any department. "Hey, Cooper." His voice shakes, and I immediately feel secondhand embarrassment for him. "Nice job tonight."

Cooper doesn't respond. It's an uncomfortable and awkward stare down. When Cooper finally opens his mouth, I hold my breath, readying myself to intervene.

"Thanks, it's nice to be able to see the whole crowd from up there."

It's a warning, we all feel it, and my mind battles on whether to say something smartass about him not having any right to watch over me or to keep my mouth shut so the night isn't ruined. I choose the latter and promise myself a brawl tomorrow.

With a smug grin, Cooper takes one of the red solo cups from Parker, tips his head back, and gulps the contents. "Did you drive?" The question is for me, but his eyes are still on Parker.

I shake my head no, although Coop can't see me. Parker is a stone.

"She's not twenty-one. You know that, right?"

Parker nods and the little respect I had for him is lost for not at least trying to stand up for himself or his date. Without asking, Cooper grabs the second cup from Parker and takes it with him, setting it down on the amp next to his guitar. One day, I'm sure I'll be thankful for Cooper watching my back, making sure my date isn't drunk when he drives me home. But the medley of emotions swerving recklessly through me right now are numbing my common sense and jacking up my stupidity.

"Damn him," I quietly grumble. I'm in full-on pout mode and can't pull it together.

Parker shoves his hands deep into his jean pockets and glances at me. "There's another party down the street. Wanna check it out?"

I'm completely turned off by my so-called date. The way he's standing, the plaid shirt that he must've gotten when he joined the hipster club along with at least thirty other plaid shirt laden dudes here tonight, and even the way he smells— like he marinated in a bottle of cologne from the same store he bought the shirt from. I'm not normally this picky, but my inner bitch is clawing her way out and Parker doesn't deserve it.

I decide to give him an easy out. "Nah, I'm going to stay and watch Cooper's band. You should go if you want."

"You sure?" He doesn't even seem disappointed that I'm not leaving with him. Quick glances around the room give away his eagerness to leave, and I'm recalling Cooper's statement about him. *Parker shit-head Travis?* I no longer feel sorry for him. Maybe he is a douche.

"Sure, Coop'll take me home. No worries. Go have fun." I flash a bright smile, relieving him of the guilt he should be feeling for leaving his date behind. Guess he's not the sweet guy he used to be. Somewhere along the road he must've drank the typical dude Kool-Aid. He's checked out and moved on already, I can see it in the way his eyes are on me but looking past me, through me, for the next game. I'm a magnet for assholes. *Ugh.*

Parker chuckles and knocks my arm with his elbow. "I was kidding, Briley. I'm not leaving you here." He's stiff, but his attention returns to the band. Being the fickle pickle that I am, I'm more pissed that he's decided to stay.

After a while, I loosen up and start singing along to some of the songs. I'm stone cold sober but managing to have a great time. Cooper's killing it on stage, his fingers hitting each chord while his right hand strums the pick along the strings. I'm in awe as I watch him. Even during Ryan's drum solo I can't take my eyes off Cooper. The way he smiles when he's up there, in his element, all of my anger and embarrassment vanishes and I know we'll be okay.

As long as we never cross that line again.

At six minutes until midnight, the band is playing "New Year's Day" by U2. I love this song and Parker and I both sing every lyric.

Three minutes until midnight, servers are handing out plastic champagne flutes to everyone in the bar, me included. No one is looking for hand stamps as everyone gets to bring in the new year with a toast. The band is covering "Learn to Fly" by Foo Fighters.

Two minutes until midnight and I look over at Parker. It's tradition to kiss someone at midnight, especially if you're on a date. Though I've never participated in this tradition because I've been at the annual party since I was a kid and my options were limited to family and friends.

Sixty seconds until midnight and I'm starting to freak out. The lyrics are pushing me to start new, find my wings and learn to fly, and I know for a fact Parker will not be part of that. I don't want to give him the wrong idea by kissing him. Besides, I have no desire to kiss him. His lips aren't appealing at all to me, and I'm suspicious of the way he probably tastes, like mint gum trying to mask the taste of cigarette smoke. I know he smokes, even though he tries to hide it by sneaking off to the bathroom several times throughout the night.

Thirty seconds until the New Year and my foot taps nervously to the same anxious rhythm as my heartbeat. The crowd is stirred up, electric with the promise of toasts, resolutions, and lips locked with their significant other. It's inevitable, I'm going to have to kiss Parker and do my best not to make a face.

There's only twenty seconds left in this year when the band ends their last song and they announce to the crowd that it's almost time to ring in the New Year.

Ryan, on the drums, starts the countdown when there's only ten seconds left.

"Ten," he shouts and taps his drumstick on the cymbal. My shoulders are tense.

"Nine." Shit.

"Eight." *It's one kiss. It doesn't mean anything.*

"Seven." This isn't how I wanted to start the New Year. Disappointment fills me as I think of all the things that have gone wrong for me this year.

"Six." It's odd, but I'm thinking about my mother and wondering if she's having a good time at the Sterlings.

"Five." The crowd is going wild, excited to start a fresh year.

"Four." I can't see Cooper, or the stage at all, and I wonder if he's going to kiss Bubblegum-Lips or Denim-Painted-Legs.

"Three." I see the look on Parker's face. He licks his lips, ready for the kiss. I hope he's used to disappointment, because a peck is the most he's getting from me.

"Two." My resolution is to do better in school. And be nicer to my mom, maybe call and come home more often. I really do like spending time with her, and the drive isn't bad at all. I'll also try to be more truthful. It's so much easier than lying.

"One." I feel a tug on my arm. The place is so packed with intoxicated celebrators, we're all bumping into each other.

"Mine," a voice demands, and I see one hand holding Parker at a distance while the other grips my arm and twirls me around to face him. "Happy New Year, B." I'm surprised I can hear him over the crowd, but somehow he's the only voice I hear. He's the only person in the room as our eyes lock, mine filled with question and hope.

He doesn't wait for permission or question whether it's a good idea to cross the line again. I know it's a bad idea, but I don't move to stop him. Instead I welcome his perfect, full lips as they crash into mine. My hands reach up, clasping behind his sweat-soaked head as we ring in the New Year, confetti floating in the air around us, lips locked and inhibitions disregarded. Nothing matters in this perfect moment except us. The way he makes me feel, the warmth that spreads through my limbs, and the faultless trust I have for this man is all I need, all I'll ever want.

When Cooper pulls back, he flashes a cocky smile before getting serious on me. "I want to be your first, B, I do. But only when the time is right." He kisses my lips softly and presses his forehead to mine. "More importantly, I want to be your last."

We stay in this position for a while as I let his words sink in. They are important words, ones that will take me a lifetime to truly understand and fully appreciate. I have nothing to say that can compare with the promises he's just made to me, so I press my lips to his again and bring in the New Year the way it was intended all along, with my best friend, the man I will love for the rest of my days, Cooper Sterling.

If you enjoyed Cooper and Briley's story, you can read more about them in the LoveStruck Series. *Wait for Me* and *Stay with Me* are available in eBook and paperback.

* Keep flipping for a sneak peek of *Wait for Me.*

ABOUT THE AUTHOR

Eleanor Green writes New Adult and Contemporary Romance swirled with mystery.

She currently lives just outside of Nashville, Tennessee with her husband and two children.

CONTACT ELEANOR

authoreleanorgreen.com

contact@authoreleanorgreen.com

Wait for Me

One

Briley

Standing tall, I filled my lungs with air before exiting the bathroom. I needed to gather my wits, or I was going to lose it. This was the last time he was doing this to me. When I came out, I stared into Blake's puffy, I've-had-too-much-to-drink, blue eyes.

He opened his mouth to speak, but I held up a hand, cutting him off. The wall behind him tried to distract me—framed memories of the two of us together, happy as we tried to build a life and home—but I clenched my fists and refocused.

"I'm going out. I'll be gone for an hour." My voice was shaky which only made me angrier. "When I return, I expect you and whatever you can pack in that amount of time to be gone." Turning on my heels, I stormed toward the front door.

"Don't you walk away from me." Blake grabbed my arm and stood in front of me, blocking my path. "Let's talk about this." He scrubbed his hands over his face, then let them fall to his sides. He was putting on a show, trying to show me his vulnerability.

I wanted to laugh. Instead I just shook my head at the man before me. My shoulders slumped with disappointment, disgust. It was hard to determine which was worse: his actions or the fact that I allowed him to do this to me . . . again.

Twenty-five was too young for bags under the eyes, but no matter how many times I replayed these last two years, I couldn't find the unpredictable fault line. Our relationship had been as close to the fairy tale I had ever dreamed possible, or so I thought. Sure, like every couple, we'd had moments, arguing over the silly stuff. I took a moment now to let a few of the memories skip through my brain.

"Do you have to paint your fingernails in here? That stuff smells." *He scrunched his nose, the few freckles that dotted it, disappearing between the creases.*

"I was here first and I'm all set up." *I waved a hand over my display.*

"Well, the game's on and this is the only room with cable." *The whoosh of air escaping a can of beer let me know he wasn't moving.*

"Fine," *I muttered, instantly pissed off. I had every intention of raking the entire contents onto the floor, but I knew who'd be cleaning it up . . . moi. Blake didn't care if the mess stayed there until Christmas.*

We got on each other's nerves on occasion, but always laughed and apologized before things got too heated. Now the question that loomed over me like a black cloud was . . . how could the man who couldn't keep his hands off me on

Tuesday, cheat on me by Friday? I'd been so sure our relationship was solid.

I'd thought that's where Blake and I were.

Heartbroken over the last few months and on the verge of crumbling, I stood strong while he overcame his demons. I had everything lined up. Our wedding was scheduled for June, then I had planned to conceive the following March.

Thankfully I found out about Blake's infidelities *before* we were married, and thank God I was faithful about taking my pill. I wasn't keen on sharing the father of my children with half the women over at Charlie's Pool & Bar.

"Bee—" Blake looked miserable. I couldn't tell if it was heartache or desperation darkening his usually clear blue eyes.

"Don't!" I pointed a warning finger close to his face. "Don't ever call me that." My mom was the only one who would ever call me "Bee" now. She'd started it in middle school when I became obsessed with honey bees.

Hers were the arms I needed to crumble into. Part of me hoped she didn't kill him when she learned how he had hurt me, but another part of me hoped she didn't look at me with pity. And finally, the strongest part of me prayed she didn't say those four dreaded words that I deserved—"I told you so." Of course my mom wouldn't say it, but if my bleary eyes ever cleared, I'd see it in her expression.

Blake took me by the shoulders, leaning down to make eye contact. "Please don't do this."

"YOU did this, Blake!" I wiggled out of his grip and turned for the kitchen. Pulling a glass from the cabinet, I filled it with ice and poured in a healthy amount of

Glenfiddich that Blake bought on a recent business trip. It was expensive, something we only pulled out on special occasions, but I didn't care. The liquid was smooth as it traveled down my throat and warmed every inch of my body. I winced from the bitter aftertaste and strong resemblance to liquid fire before gulping the rest down.

"Yes, I did this." His shoulders slumped with what I could only imagine was deep regret. "Give me a chance to make things right again."

"You're out of chances, Blake. No more nice girl." Unlike the past, I was serious this time.

He held out a hand, but instantly withdrew it when he saw me wince. "You *are* a nice girl. Kind, giving . . . the peacemaker. So damn sweet, it's one of the reasons I fell in love with you."

"Bullshit!" I spun around, my long dark hair swishing against my back. "You've never fallen in love with anyone but yourself. I was a sucker and you're a thief!" My blood boiled in my veins, my stomach churning. I swallowed hard before continuing. "You took what you wanted and trampled it." I squared my shoulders, trying hard to look tougher than I felt. "But don't you worry about me. I've studied you and all the ways a snake can disguise himself. I'll benefit from this."

Somehow, one day.

"I'm begging you . . . I love you." Pain flickered in his eyes. "Together—"

I shook my head. This was over and I was done listening. "Save your blubbering for someone who actually gives a crap, honey. I've heard Andi prefers leftovers—she can comfort you now." My words spewed like venom, the poison visibly affecting his mood.

His eyebrows narrowed, finally revealing his true nature. He had lost and knew it. Like a little boy that didn't get the toy he saw on the store shelf, I wondered if he'd throw himself on the floor, or worse. He'd never hit me before, but I'd never seen his eyes darken this much. His pupils were so large, the only visible blue was a fine navy circle around deep pools of wrath. With clenched fists, he leaned toward me. I flinched, my body tense and ready to take a blow. It didn't come, but the threat had done its job in shaking me.

Scotch on an empty stomach was never a good idea and the buzz hit me hard. Trying to keep my shoulders back in confidence as I walked away was more challenging than I had anticipated. I gripped the counter, regaining my balance and strutted out of the house like a drunken goose.

Blake was right behind me, but I kept moving forward, refusing to acknowledge his presence.

"You can't drive, Bee—Briley." He clutched my arm, digging into the flesh until I grimaced. "You've been drinking."

"I know that," I hissed. Jerking my arm loose, I turned and glared at him through narrowed, furious eyes. "Drinking makes you do stupid things. Like throwing your life away for a ten-minute roll in the sheets."

With impeccable timing, my mother pulled into the driveway. I'd texted her three pound signs—my get out of jail free code from high school—and prayed she'd remember what it meant.

Blake huffed and ran an angry hand through his thick, blond hair. "You called Nina?"

Without answering, or looking at him, I stepped into the car and managed not to slam the door. Cool as a cucumber, I buckled my seatbelt and pretended to fish through my purse for a piece of gum. I could sense my mom's anger penetrating Blake through the window even though I hadn't told her anything. She could always read me like a book and knew everything that was going on in my life without either of us speaking a word. I waited until she was out of the driveway and around the corner before I released the sob that played at my throat.

Sucking in high-pitched breaths between words, I tried to explain. I was sure none of it was intelligible, but knowing my mom, she got it.

"I need . . . to see . . . Cooper." My words came out choppy and sounded like I had a nose full of cotton.

"You know it's not possible, honey." My mother white-knuckled the steering wheel, revealing the depth of her anger. It must've been difficult to watch your child go through something so traumatic and feel completely helpless.

"It *is* possible," I argued. "He doesn't want me there, but I *need* him. Surely he can understand that."

www.ingramcontent.com/pod-product-compliance
Lightning Source LLC
Chambersburg PA
CBHW020558130626
46552CB00007B/2942